Taking Your Camera to JAPAN

Ted Park

Raintree Steck-Vaughn Publishers
A Harcourt Company
Austin · New York
www.steck-vaughn.com

Published by Raintree Steck-Vaughn Publishers,
an imprint of Steck-Vaughn Company

Library of Congress Cataloging-in-Publication Data
Park, Ted
    Japan / by Ted Park.
        p. cm. — (Taking your camera to)
    Summary: Introduces the geography, points of interest, way of life, economy, culture, and people of Japan.
    ISBN 0-7398-1805-8
    1. Japan—Juvenile literature. [1. Japan.] I. Title: Japan. II. Series.

DS806.P375 2000
952—dc21   99-058640

Printed in the United States of America
10 9 8 7 6 5 4 3 2 1 W 03 02 01 00

Photo acknowledgments

Cover ©FPG International; p.1 ©Travelpix/FPG International; p.3a ©Michael S. Yamashita/CORBIS; p.3b ©Keren Su/FPG International; p.3c ©VCG/FPG Interntational; p.3d ©David Samuel Robbins/CORBIS; p.5 ©Telegraph Colour Library/FPG International; p.8 ©Keren Su/FPG International; p.9 ©Michael S. Yamashita/CORBIS; p.11 ©Ken Ross/FPG International; p.13a ©Harvey Lloyd/FPG International; p.13b ©David Samuel Robbins/CORBIS; p.15a ©Travelpix/FPG International; p.15b ©VCG/FPG Interntational; p.17 ©Natalie Fobes/CORBIS; p.19a ©Travelpix/FPG International; p.19b ©Harvey Lloyd/FPG International; p.21 ©Jean Kugler/FPG International; pp.23, 25, 27a ©Travelpix/FPG International; p.27b ©VCG/FPG International; p.28a ©Ken Ross/FPG International; p.28b ©Keren Su/FPG International; p.29a ©PhotoDisc; p.29b ©Michael S. Yamashita/CORBIS; p.29c ©Jean Kugler/FPG International.

All statistics in the Quick Facts section come from *The New York Times Almanac* (1999) and *The World Almanac* (1999).

96619

Contents

This Is Japan 4

The Place 6

Tokyo 10

Places to Visit 12

The People 14

Life in Japan 16

Government and Religion 18

Earning a Living 20

School and Sports 22

Food and Holidays 24

The Future 26

Quick Facts About Japan 28

Glossary 30

Index 32

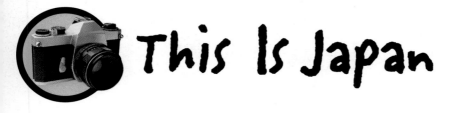# This Is Japan

Japan is one of the oldest countries in the world. Its history goes back thousands of years. If you took your camera to Japan, you could photograph many old things. Japan has many temples and shrines. These are places where Japanese people go to worship. Some of these places are hundreds of years old.

In the past, Japanese people wore kimonos. A kimono is a long robe that is tied together with a piece of cloth. Now many Japanese wear modern clothes.

Japan is also a very modern country. It has many big cities. One of them is Tokyo, the capital of Japan. Tokyo is also the largest city in Japan.

Japan is a mixture of old and new. This book will show you some of each. It will also tell you much about the country of Japan. If you learn about Japan before you take your camera there, you will enjoy your visit more.

Although Japan is a very old country, it is also very modern. It has many large cities with big buildings.

The Place

Japan is a country off the east coast of Asia. To the east of Japan is the Pacific Ocean. To the west is the Sea of Japan.

Japan is made up of four large islands and 3,000 smaller ones. When all the islands of Japan are put together, Japan is 1,300 miles (2,092 km) long. This is about the size of the state of California.

No part of Japan is more than 75 miles (121 km) from the sea. Most people live near the coasts. There are small rivers and lakes. Almost three-fourths of Japan has forests. There are many valleys. There is not much flat land in Japan. Because of this, there is not much farming.

Japan has many mountains. They are mostly on the west coast. Many of these mountains are volcanoes. The best known volcano is Mount Fuji. It is 12,385 feet (3,776 m) tall. It is also Japan's highest mountain. Mount Fuji has not erupted since 1707.

 6

Japan often has earthquakes. Some of them are hardly felt. But some are very strong. Japan has had many strong earthquakes in the 20th century. The most recent one was in 1995. It damaged the city of Kobe very badly. Many buildings were destroyed.

Mount Fuji is one of Japan's most famous sites.

In Japan, most of the people live along the seacoast.

The climate in the northern part of Japan is cool. It is warmer in the south. In the fall typhoons may hit Japan. These are storms that have strong winds and heavy rain. Japan may have as many as 30 typhoons a year. During a typhoon, winds can be as high as 124 miles (199 km) an hour. There may be as much as 12 inches (30 cm) of rain in one day.

9 📷

Tokyo

The capital of Japan is Tokyo. Most of Tokyo is very modern. Tokyo is located on the Kanto Plain on the island of Honshu. Almost 8 million people live in the city itself. But more than 30 million people live around the center of the city.

The streets of Tokyo are crowded. There are many traffic jams. Buildings are often crowded together. Because of this, many people live in very small houses. Many people live in apartments in tall buildings.

Tokyo has a main shopping street. It is called the Ginza. To the west of the Ginza is the business district. To the east there are homes. These parts of Tokyo are joined by a fast subway system.

Tokyo was destroyed by a big earthquake in 1923. More than 100,000 people died, many in fires. Because so many buildings were ruined, Tokyo had to be rebuilt. Now Tokyo has tall skyscrapers. They are made so they will not be damaged during earthquakes.

The Ginza at night

 10

Places to Visit

Kyoto is one of the largest cities in Japan. It is on the island of Honshu. Kyoto was once the capital of Japan. One of the most famous places in Kyoto is the Imperial Palace. This is where the shoguns lived. Shoguns were strong military leaders who ruled Japan. The palace is surrounded by parks and gardens.

In the city of Hiroshima there is a peace monument. A monument is a thing that was made to remind people of something important. The peace monument reminds people that war is bad. It was made after World War II.

Sapporo is a city on the island of Hokkaido. People come to Sapporo from all around the world to ski down its snowy mountains. The 1972 Winter Olympic Games were held at Sapporo.

**The Gold Pavilion
in Kyoto**

**The peace monument
in Hiroshima**

13 📷

The People

About 126 million people live in Japan. Almost all of them are Japanese. Very few people who live in Japan are not Japanese.

Early settlers to Japan probably came from northern Asia. Later ones came from Korea and China. Many of the Chinese settlers brought their customs with them. In fact, the Japanese system of writing came from China. It is made up of signs. Many of these signs stand for words, not sounds. But over time, Chinese customs faded.

When the first settlers came from Asia, they found people already living in Japan. These are the Ainu. A small number of Ainu still live in Japan. They mostly live on the island of Hokkaido. The Ainu have their own language. They also have their own way of living. Because of this, many of them feel left out of modern Japanese life.

This young girl is wearing old-time Japanese clothes.

Most Japanese, like these businesspeople, wear modern clothes.

15 📷

 # Life in Japan

Most Japanese live in large cities. Many of them live in small apartments. Many of these people have moved from the countryside. Young people go to cities to find jobs.

Many homes in Japan are very simple and very clean. There are no rugs on the floors. Instead there are usually straw mats. These are called tatami mats. There may be a low table in the center of the main room. In Japan, the people may sleep on futons. These are small mattresses that can be rolled up and put away during the day. If you were invited into a Japanese house, there would be one room that you might recognize. It is the kitchen. A kitchen in a Japanese home will look like a kitchen in a home in the United States.

The Japanese way of life is very old. The Japanese people often try to live with the old as well as the new.

The Japanese tea ceremony takes place in a simple room.

One old Japanese custom is the tea ceremony. It takes place in a simple room. People make and then drink tea. While they do this, they try to think of nothing else. They try to feel peaceful while the tea ceremony takes place.

 Government and Religion

The head of the Japanese government is the emperor. An emperor is a person who rules over a very large area. But all the work in the government is done by other people. These people are elected by the people of Japan. This type of government is called a constitutional monarchy. A group of people makes the laws. This group is called the Diet. It is made up of two smaller groups. They are the House of Representatives and the House of Councillors. The Diet chooses the prime minister. This person runs the country.

Japan has two main religions. They are Buddhism and Shinto. Buddhism began in India and came to Japan in the 6th century A.D.

18

The Shinto religion began in Japan and is found nowhere else. There are many Shinto shrines throughout the country. Almost every town and city has a shrine. People go to the shrines to pray for what they want or need. Many Japanese pin pieces of paper with prayers written on them onto Shinto shrines. Many Japanese believe in both religions.

This is a statue of Buddha, who started the religion of Buddhism. ▼

There are many shrines ▲ throughout Japan.

Earning a Living

Japan makes many things that people all over the world use. These include cameras, television sets, and computers. Japan also makes cars. In fact, Japan is the largest car maker in the world. One-third of all cars made come from Japan. So does one-third of all steel and ships. Two-thirds of all computer chips and electronic products are made in Japan. Most of these parts are put together by electronic workers, robots.

There are very few farms in Japan. And these farms are very small. Rice is the most important crop. It is also the main food of the Japanese. Some vegetables are grown. Mulberry trees are also grown. The Japanese feed mulberry leaves to silkworms. These insects make silk, for which Japan is famous.

Because much of Japan is near the sea, fishing is an important industry. Japan has more fishing boats than any other country.

Robots putting cars together in a Japanese factory

21 📷

School and Sports

In Japan young people have to go to school from ages 6 to 16. Most of them stay in school until they are 18. Then one-third of them go to college. Japanese schools are good at teaching many subjects, especially math and science. Lessons are very hard. Exams that are taken to get into schools are hard, too.

Most young Japanese people like sports. Judo is popular in Japan. Kendo is also well known. Kendo is a sport in which players strike each other with bamboo or wooden sticks. Baseball is a very popular team sport. The game was brought to Japan from the United States. Soccer is another team sport that is becoming popular. Japanese people also enjoy sumo wrestling. They watch large wrestlers try to make each other touch the ground or go outside a certain area.

Japanese enjoy playing on the snowy mountain slopes at Sapporo.

 22

 # Food and Holidays

Japanese people eat fish at almost every meal. Raw fish dishes are very popular. Sushi is a delicious dish made of pieces of raw fish and rice that are rolled inside dried seaweed. Another favorite is sashimi. Sashimi is made of pieces of raw fish that are dipped in a spicy sauce. Another popular dish is a delicious soup called miso. This is made from dried soybeans that are mashed and then mixed with broth.

The Japanese eat three times as much fish as meat. But beef is also popular.

The most important holiday of the year to the Japanese is New Year's Day. It is on January 1. The Japanese decorate their homes. They visit friends, and give gifts and eat special foods. In May Children's Day is celebrated. It is a national holiday. A flag in the shape of a fish is hung outdoors. The fish stands for energy.

Many other holidays take place in Japan throughout

 24

During some Japanese festivals, people wear special clothes.

the year. There may be parades and floats during them.
There may also be dancing and singing.

25 📷

# The Future

If you took your camera to Japan, you could take photos of an important industrial country. An industrial country is one that makes a lot of goods. Because of this industry, there are plenty of jobs in Japan.

However, like other countries, Japan has some problems. Although Japan's fast Bullet trains are popular, there are many cars on the roads of Japan. They can pollute the air. Some of the Japanese industries can pollute the air, too.

Many, many people live in Japan. But the country only grows about half of the food it needs. The rest must be imported, or brought, in from other places. Some of these things cost a lot of money.

The people of Japan are proud of their country. They are excited about the future of Japan. When you leave Japan, someone may say "Sayonara" to you. In English, this means "Good-bye."

When you take your camera to Japan, you can visit the stock exchange in Tokyo. You can also take a ride on a fast Bullet train.

Quick Facts About
JAPAN

Capital
Tokyo

Borders
Sea of Okhotsk to the north; East
China Sea to the southwest; Sea of
Japan to the west; Pacific Ocean to
the east

Area
145,882 square miles
(377,805 sq km)

Population
125,931,533

Largest Cities
Tokyo (7,836,665 people);
Yokohama (3,273,609 people);
Osaka (2,478,628 people)

Chief crops
rice, sugar beets, vegetables

Natural resources
almost none

Longest river
Shinono, 228 miles (367 km)

28

Flag of Japan

◀ **Coastline**
18,487 miles (29,751 km)

Monetary unit
yen

Literacy rate
100 percent of the Japanese people can read and write

Major industries
engineering; electric, car, steel, and electronic industries; shipbuilding; fishing

29

Glossary

Ainu (EYE-noo) The first people who lived in Japan

Buddhism (BOO-diz-uhm) A religion that began in India and spread to Japan in the 6th century A.D.

Bullet trains Fast Japanese trains

constitutional monarchy (kahn-stu-TOO-shun-uhl MAHN-ur-kee) A type of government in which a king or emperor is the head of the country but the work of governing is done by people who were elected

Diet (Deye-ut) The group of people that makes the laws in Japan

emperor (EM-pur-ur) The head of the Japanese government

futon (FOO-tahn) A small mattress on which the Japanese sleep

Ginza (GEEN-zuh) Tokyo's main shopping street

Hiroshima (hir-uh-SHEE-muh) A city in Japan where the United States dropped an atomic bomb during World War II

Hokkaido (hah-KEED-oh) The most northern island in Japan

Honshu (HAHN-shoo) The Japanese island on which Tokyo and Kyoto are located

judo (JOOD-oh) A sport that is similar to wrestling

kendo (KEN-doh) A sport in which players strike each other with bamboo or wooden sticks

kimono (kuh-MOW-noh) A long robe tied with a piece of cloth

Kyoto (kee-OH-toe) The capital of ancient Japan

miso (MEE-sow) A soup made from mashed soybeans and broth

Mount Fuji (FOO-jee) Japan's highest mountain

Sapporo (SAH-pour-oh) The Japanese city in which the 1972 Winter Olympic Games were held.

sashimi (SAHSH-uh-mee) A popular Japanese dish made of pieces of raw fish dipped in a spicy sauce

Shinto (SHIN-tow) A religion found only in Japan

shogun (SHOW-gun) A strong military leader

sumo wrestling (SOO-mow) A sport in which wrestlers try to make each other touch the ground or go outside a certain area

sushi (SOO-shee) A popular Japanese dish made of pieces of raw fish and rice rolled inside dried seaweed

tatami mat (tah-TAHM-ee) A straw floor mat

Tokyo (TOW-kee-oh) The capital of Japan, and its largest city

typhoons (ty-FOONZ) Storms with strong winds and heavy rainfall

31

Index

Ainu 14
Asia 6, 14

Buddhism 18
Bullet trains 26

Children's Day 24
China 14
constitutional monarchy 18

Diet 18

futons 16

Ginza 10

Hiroshima 12
Hokkaido 14
Honshu 10

Imperial Palace 12

judo 22

kendo 22
kimono 4
Kyoto 12

miso 24
Mount Fuji 6

New Year's Day 24

Pacific Ocean 6

sashimi 24
Sea of Japan 6
Shinto 18
shogun 12
sumo wrestling 22
sushi 24

tatami mats 16
Tokyo 4, 10

United States 16

World War II 12, 16